Timon of
Athens

Sweet Cherry

Published by Sweet Cherry Publishing Limited
Unit 36, Vulcan House,
Vulcan Road,
Leicester, LE5 3EF
United Kingdom

First published in the US in 2013
2020 hardback edition

2 4 6 8 10 9 7 5 3

ISBN: 978-1-78226-730-0

©Macaw Books

Timon of Athens

Lexile® code numerical measure L = Lexile® 1210L

Guided Reading Level = T

Cover design and illustrations by Macaw Books

www.sweetcherrypublishing.com

Printed and bound in India
I.TP002

About Shakespeare

William Shakespeare, regarded as the greatest writer in the English language, was born in Stratford-upon-Avon in Warwickshire, England, in 1564. He was the third of eight children born to John and Mary Shakespeare.

Shakespeare was a poet, playwright and dramatist. He is often known as England's national poet and the "Bard of Avon." Thirty-eight plays, one hundred and fifty-four sonnets, two long narrative poems and several other poems are attributed to him. Shakespeare's plays have been translated into every major existent language and are performed more often than those of any other playwright.

Timon: Timon is a wealthy man in Athens, who likes to throw lavish feasts for his friends and send them gifts. But when he goes bankrupt, everyone deserts him. Then he goes into the forest, hating humanity.

Flavius: He is the loyal servant of Timon. He repeatedly tries to warn his master not to spend so much money, but his words fall on deaf ears. He even goes in search of Timon in the forest, but is sent back by Timon with harsh words.

Ventidius: He is a young Athenian whom Timon helped to get out of

prison. However, he refuses to help Timon when Timon goes bankrupt.

Alcibiades: He is a soldier who has raised an army to destroy Athens. He meets Timon in the forest, who supports Alcibiades. In a way, Alcibiades tries to right the wrong that has been done to Timon.

Timon of Athens

Once upon a time, there was a lord in Athens by the name of Timon. Though he was very wealthy, Timon had a tendency to spend much more

than he actually had. He would not spend much of it on himself, but rather, would spend his fortune on all kinds of people—be it the poor people of the city or even other wealthy lords like himself. His house would always be open to everyone and grand meals would always be prepared for anyone who might want to visit at any time of the day. Even the rich people of the town would deflate their egos and go to Timon for a feast. There was not a

single person on the streets
of Athens who had not
been under the patronage
of the great Timon.

He would commission
unworthy poets, buy
paintings from painters
which were not being
sold to anyone else in the
city and persuade jewelers
to sell him high-priced
stones which no one else
could buy. Anything
and everything which
required his wealth to help
another person was done
and he cast no distinction
between anybody.

A large number of people who lived as Timon's dependents were actually young men from rich households, who had been thrown into prison by their creditors for the nonpayment of loans, and Timon would immediately get them out of jail. One such spendthrift was a man called Ventidius, for whom Timon had recently paid a huge sum to absolve him of his debts.

But Timon did not realize that all these men

were interested in was his wealth, not his companionship. They would all cherish the moment when Timon took a fancy to anything that belonged to them, for they would then charge him an exorbitant amount for the item. Some people would even

send him things that
he had commented
on some time ago.
They knew that
Timon would accept their gifts
and return their "generosity"
with a more expensive gift
or, in most cases, money.

But it was not that Timon only spent his wealth on such people. He would also act as a philanthropist in noble and praiseworthy acts. For instance, one day his servant came to him and declared that he had fallen in love with a rich Athenian's daughter. However,

he knew he could never express
his love for her because of his
poor and pitiable condition.
Timon immediately gave the
servant a huge amount
of money, making
him rich beyond
his wildest dreams
and enabling

him to marry the love of his life. However, such acts were few in number, as most of the

people who fed off his wealth were spendthrifts, who managed to increase their own fortunes by misleading the noble Timon.

Timon never considered that his wealth might soon be gone due to how much he was spending. His steward, Flavius, a rather honest fellow, would

often try to bring it to his master's attention, but Timon would always succeed in changing the topic to something more frivolous. He paid no heed to his steward's genuine words, but rather doted on the false exaggerations of his flatterers. Every night, when the rooms of his house were

full of freeloaders,
drinking his
wine like water,
Flavius would
retire to a solitary
corner and cry his heart out
over his master's foolish ways.

But one day, Timon was
forced to face reality. He ordered

Flavius to sell some more of his land to meet his payments, only for Flavius to inform him that most of the land he owned was either already sold or had been forfeited. What he had at that moment was not even worth a third of the debts he had incurred. Timon tried to

explain to him that he had lands from Athens to Lacedaemon, but Flavius only replied, "O my good lord, the world is but a world, and has bounds; were it all yours to give in a breath, how quickly were it gone!"

But Timon managed to console the weeping Flavius by telling him that all was not lost. After all, he had not made unwise decisions regarding his expenses, but had spent the money on his friends, who would now surely take care of him. He sent

Flavius to the houses of various lords who had once been the recipients of Timon's generosity and asked them to lend him money. He also sent his noble steward to the house of Ventidius, the young man whom he had rescued from prison, to ask for the return of the money he had paid previously. After all, Ventidius's father had died recently, leaving his son ample wealth. Timon was confident

that when his friends received
the message, they would open
their coffers and pay him up to
five hundred times the amount
of money he had asked for.

Flavius first arrived at
the house of Lord Lucullus,
a wealthy man who had been
feasting off Timon his whole life.
He had long been dreaming of

a silver cup, and the minute he
was told that Timon's servant
had called upon him, he thought
his dream had come true and
that Timon must have sent him
the silver cup he had cherished
for so long. But when he heard

the true nature of Flavius's visit, he at once made a song and dance about how he had always warned Timon of his spending habits. He had supposedly come to dinner many a time with the request that such dinners should

not be had, as they would one day come back to haunt Timon. And of course, when he could not conclude his argument at these dinners, he would come back for breakfast and lunch the following day and continue with his speech. Finally, he ended

his whole soliloquy by trying to bribe Flavius, so that the honest steward could go home and tell his master that he had not been able to meet Lucullus at home.

There was little success at the house of Lord Lucius, who still lay in bed after the hearty dinner he had consumed at

Timon's house the night before. When he heard the news and realized that the winds had changed,  he lost no time in crying over Timon's fate. However, he had made a rather hefty purchase the day before, and was now in no

position to repay his generous friend and pull him out of the dire straits he was in. He kept up the pretense of crying and rebuking himself for not being able to help a friend who had always showered him with gifts and affection.

It was the same story throughout the city of Athens. Every house Flavius went to came up with the same story—they

wanted to help their friend,
but for some reason or other
they were unable to. Even the
ungrateful Ventidius refused to
pay the money his friend had
so generously given him to get

him out of prison, even though
he now had plenty to do so.

Timon's house, once a place
where everybody would stop
and go inside, had now become
somewhere people would just
walk past, perhaps even run,
in the event that Timon might

spot them and come out to ask
for money. The only people
who came to visit Timon now
were his cold-hearted creditors,
who would thrust bills before
him and ask him to pay the
amounts requested. Timon's
house was now like a prison,
a place he could neither stay

in nor leave until his dues had been paid.

However, there was the last act of the setting sun that had to be carried out. All the lords who were avoiding Timon like the plague were suddenly bewildered to find themselves invited to a feast at his house. They all thought that he had merely pretended to be poor to test their love for him. But they were happy that Timon was now back to his old self and soon they would be able to rip

him off like they had done
so many times before.

So, when the
declared date arrived,
all the lords and ladies,
dressed in their finery,
made their way to
Timon's house to partake
in the festivities. When
they arrived, they saw

that everything was back to
normal and it was as if Timon
had never been poor at all. They
all wondered how a poor man
had been able to arrange such
a gala feast when
suddenly, the food
appeared. Alas, all
that was being
served was smoke

and lukewarm water. It was
Timon's way of showing his
"friends" what their friendship
was all about. Before the guests
realized what was happening,
Timon started to throw the
water at them, abusing them.
The guests left without another
word. Some lost portions of
their gowns, some ladies

even lost their jewelry, but no one dared to stay there for a minute longer. There was no knowing what this madman would do next!

That was the last time they ever saw Timon. He headed into the forests beyond the city walls, where he found the wild beasts more grateful than the people he had given all his wealth to. He wished that all the houses he could see on the horizon would fall, leaving those men to the same fate to

which he was now consigned. He
ate the wild roots in the forest and

drank from the streams that nature provided.

One day, as he was trying to dig up some wild roots for his meal, his spade struck something. It was a huge chest of gold, perhaps left there by some robber who could not make it back to retrieve it and was now perhaps rotting in prison. It was now in Timon's possession.

Had Timon been the Timon of old, he would be pleased he now had enough gold to buy his friends again. But the very sight of the gold disgusted

him, and he was about to bury the chest when he decided he could use it for something worthwhile.

A group of Athenian soldiers, under the leadership of General Alcibiades, had been camping near the edge of the forest. They too had faced ingratitude from

the people of the city, whom they
had defended with their lives,
and were about to march into
the city to fight the ungrateful
senators. Timon took the gold
to Alcibiades and asked him to
pay all his soldiers. All he asked
in return was that they attack

the city and kill its inhabitants,
not leaving a single soul alive
at the end of their
conquest. Timon
truly hated all
Athenians and
mankind in general.

One day, as Timon lay in
the forest, completely naked—for
he had lost all his clothes—he
saw a man standing near him,
looking on respectfully. It was
his old steward, Flavius, whose
love for his master had made him

come to the forest
looking for him.
But Timon felt that
since Flavius was a
human being, he must
also be a traitor and the tears
that he cried were false. Flavius
tried to prove to his master that

he was not like the men who had
deserted him when he needed
them the most, and he was able
to convince Timon that there
was at least one honest man left
in the world. But since he was
in the garb of a man and part
of mankind, Timon had to ask

him to leave. And that was the
last that Timon saw of Flavius.

But now the Athenians
thought of Timon again, because
besides being the friend that he
was, he had also been the general
of the army, the only man who
could resist the attacks of the
murderous Alcibiades. His men

had stormed the city and were destroying everything like wild boars. A group of senators went to the forest in search of Timon, to beg him to save them. When they found him, they tried everything they could to get Timon to agree. They promised him riches, nobility, dignities, retribution for past injuries,

everything. But Timon, the man-hater that he was, could not care less. There was no way he would ever go back to save mankind.

However, just as the weeping senators were about to leave, Timon turned to them and said that there was only one way in which the Athenians could save themselves from the

cruelty of Alcibiades. He mentioned that there was a huge tree in front of his cave, which he was about to cut down. He asked the Athenians to go to the tree and hang themselves from it. That was the only way they could save themselves from the wrath of Alcibiades!

Soon thereafter, whenever someone walked by the sea coast near the city, they would see a grave there, with an epitaph that read: *While he lived, he hated all living men, and while dying, wished a plague might consume all left!* Timon of Athens lived the rest of his life as the man-hater he had become. And what better place for his burial than the sea, so that the waters could cry for him forever!